"Yes and back again!
If your heels
Are nimble and light,
You may get there
By candlelight."

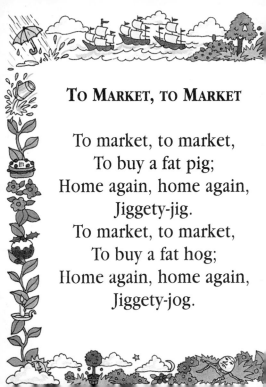

TO MARKET, TO MARKET

To market, to market,
To buy a fat pig;
Home again, home again,
Jiggety-jig.
To market, to market,
To buy a fat hog;
Home again, home again,
Jiggety-jog.

LITTLE BOY BLUE

Little Boy Blue,
Come blow your horn,
The cow's in the meadow,
The sheep's in the corn;
Where is the boy
Who looks after the sheep?
He's under the haystack
Fast asleep!

SIMPLE SIMON

Simple Simon
Met a pieman,
Going to the fair;
Says Simple Simon
To the pieman,
"Let me taste your ware."
Says the pieman
To Simple Simon,
"Show me first your penny."
Says Simple Simon
To the pieman,
"Indeed I have not any."

As I was Going to St Ives

As I was going to St Ives,
I met a man with seven wives;
Each wife had seven sacks,
Each sack had seven cats,
Each cat had seven kits:
Kits, cats, sacks, and wives,
How many were going
To St Ives?

SING A SONG OF SIXPENCE

Sing a song of sixpence,
A pocket full of rye;
Four and twenty
blackbirds
Baked in a pie;

When the pie was opened,
The birds began to sing;
Was not that a dainty dish,
To set before the king?

The king was in his
counting-house,
Counting out his money;
The queen was in the parlour
Eating bread and honey;

The maid was in the garden
Hanging out the clothes;
There came a little blackbird,
And snapped off her nose.

HICKORY, DICKORY, DOCK

Hickory, Dickory, Dock,
The mouse ran up the clock;
The clock struck one;
The mouse ran down;
Hickory, Dickory, Dock.

DIDDLE, DIDDLE, DUMPLING, MY SON JOHN

Diddle, diddle, dumpling,
My son John,
Went to bed
With his trousers on;
One shoe off,
One shoe on,
Diddle, diddle, dumpling,
My son John.

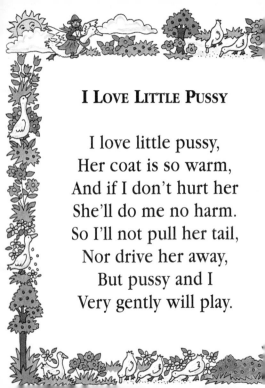

I LOVE LITTLE PUSSY

I love little pussy,
Her coat is so warm,
And if I don't hurt her
She'll do me no harm.
So I'll not pull her tail,
Nor drive her away,
But pussy and I
Very gently will play.

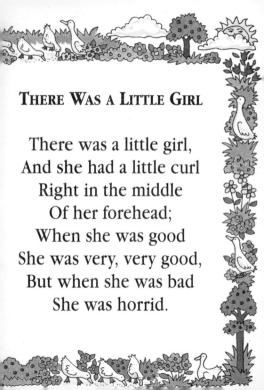

THERE WAS A LITTLE GIRL

There was a little girl,
And she had a little curl
Right in the middle
Of her forehead;
When she was good
She was very, very good,
But when she was bad
She was horrid.

A WISE OLD OWL

A wise old owl
Lived in an oak;
The more he saw
The less he spoke.
The less he spoke
The more he heard.
Why can't we all be
Like that wise old bird?

Humpty Dumpty

Humpty Dumpty
Sat on a wall;
Humpty Dumpty
Had a great fall;
All the king's horses,
And all the king's men
Couldn't put Humpty
Together again.

THREE BLIND MICE

Three blind mice,
Three blind mice,
See how they run!
See how they run!
They all ran after
The farmer's wife,
Who cut off their tails
With a carving-knife;
Did you ever see
Such fun in your life
As three blind mice?

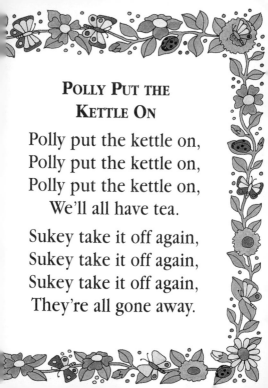

POLLY PUT THE KETTLE ON

Polly put the kettle on,
Polly put the kettle on,
Polly put the kettle on,
 We'll all have tea.

Sukey take it off again,
Sukey take it off again,
Sukey take it off again,
 They're all gone away.

BAA, BAA, BLACK SHEEP

Baa, baa, black sheep,
Have you any wool?
"Yes, sir, yes, sir,
Three bags full;
One for the master,
And one for the dame,
And one for the little boy
Who lives down the lane."

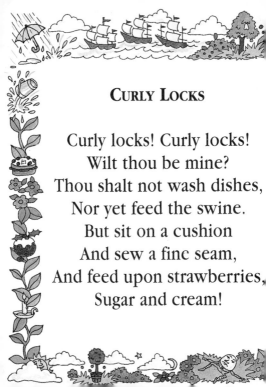

CURLY LOCKS

Curly locks! Curly locks!
Wilt thou be mine?
Thou shalt not wash dishes,
Nor yet feed the swine.
But sit on a cushion
And sew a fine seam,
And feed upon strawberries,
Sugar and cream!

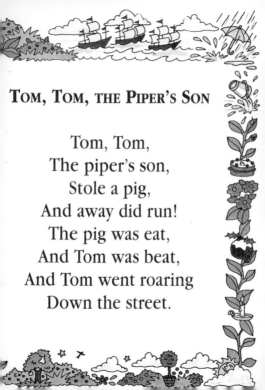

TOM, TOM, THE PIPER'S SON

Tom, Tom,
The piper's son,
Stole a pig,
And away did run!
The pig was eat,
And Tom was beat,
And Tom went roaring
Down the street.

OLD MOTHER HUBBARD

Old Mother Hubbard
Went to the cupboard
To get her poor dog a bone;
But when she came there
The cupboard was bare,
And so the poor dog had none.

RIDE A COCK-HORSE

Ride a cock-horse
To Banbury Cross,
To see a fine lady
Upon a white horse;
With rings on her fingers
And bells on her toes,
She shall have music
Wherever she goes.

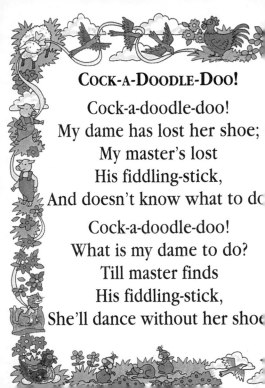

COCK-A-DOODLE-DOO!

Cock-a-doodle-doo!
My dame has lost her shoe;
My master's lost
His fiddling-stick,
And doesn't know what to do

Cock-a-doodle-doo!
What is my dame to do?
Till master finds
His fiddling-stick,
She'll dance without her shoe

Cock-a-doodle-doo!
My dame has found her shoe,
And master's found
His fiddling-stick,
Sing doodle-doodle-doo!

Cock-a-doodle-doo!
My dame will dance with you,
While master fiddles
His fiddling-stick,
For dame and doodle-doo.

IF...

If all the world
Was apple pie,
And all the sea
Was ink,
And all the trees
Were bread and cheese,
What should we have
to drink?

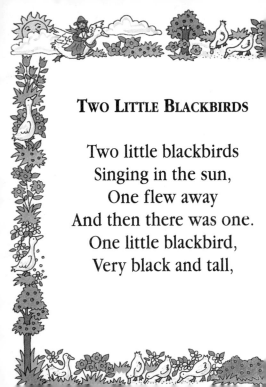

TWO LITTLE BLACKBIRDS

Two little blackbirds
Singing in the sun,
One flew away
And then there was one.
One little blackbird,
Very black and tall,

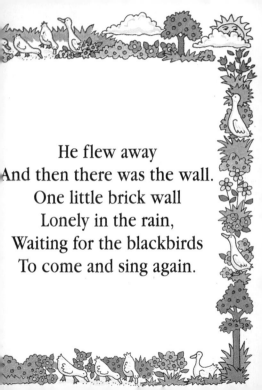

He flew away
And then there was the wall.
One little brick wall
Lonely in the rain,
Waiting for the blackbirds
To come and sing again.

RUB A DUB DUB

Rub a dub dub,
Three men in a tub;
And who do you think they be?
The butcher, the baker,
The candlestick-maker;
Turn 'em out, knaves all three.

MARY HAD A LITTLE LAMB

Mary had a little lamb,
With fleece as white as snow
And everywhere that Mary wen
The lamb was sure to go.

It followed her to school one da
Which was against the rule.
And made the children laugl
and play,
To see a lamb at school.

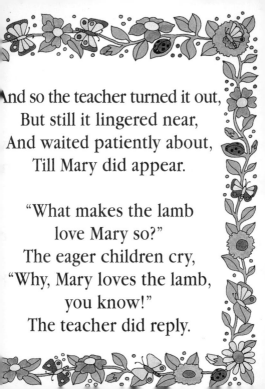

And so the teacher turned it out,
But still it lingered near,
And waited patiently about,
Till Mary did appear.

"What makes the lamb
love Mary so?"
The eager children cry,
"Why, Mary loves the lamb,
you know!"
The teacher did reply.

DING, DONG, BELL

Ding, dong, bell,
Pussy's in the well!
Who put her in?—
Little Tommy Green.
Who pulled her out?—
Little Johnny Stout.
What a naughty boy was that
To try to drown poor pussy-cat,
Who never did any harm,
But killed the mice
In his father's barn.

HOW MANY MILES TO BABYLON?

"How many miles to Babylon?"
"Three score miles and ten."
"Can I get there by candlelight?"

SIX LITTLE MICE

Six little mice
Sat down to spin.
Pussy passed by,
And she peeped in.
"What are you at,
My little men?"
"Making coats
For gentlemen."

"Shall I come in
And bite off your threads?"
"No, no Miss Pussy,
You'll snip off our heads."
"Oh, no, I'll not.
I'll help you to spin."
"That may be so,
But you can't come in!"

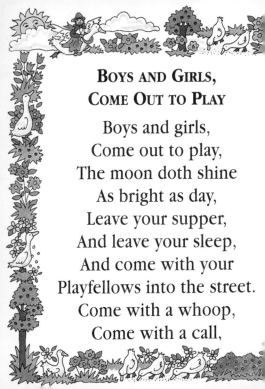

BOYS AND GIRLS, COME OUT TO PLAY

Boys and girls,
Come out to play,
The moon doth shine
As bright as day,
Leave your supper,
And leave your sleep,
And come with your
Playfellows into the street.
Come with a whoop,
Come with a call,

Come with a good will,
Or come not at all.
Up the ladder
And down the wall,
A halfpenny loaf
Will serve us all.
You find milk,
And I'll find flour,
And we'll have pudding
In half an hour.

HEY DIDDLE, DIDDLE

Hey diddle, diddle,
The cat and the fiddle,
The cow jumped over
the moon;

The little dog laughed
To see such sport,
And the dish ran away
with the spoon.

There Was a Crooked Man

There was a crooked man,
And he went a crooked mile,
He found a crooked sixpence
Against a crooked stile:
He bought a crooked cat,
Which caught a crooked mouse,
And they all lived together
In a little crooked house.

LITTLE BO-PEEP

Little Bo-Peep
Has lost her sheep,
And doesn't know
Where to find them;
Leave them alone,
And they'll come home,
Bringing their tails
Behind them.

LITTLE JACK HORNER

Little Jack Horner
Sat in a corner,
Eating a
Christmas pie;
He put in a thumb,
And pulled out a plum,
And said,
"What a good boy am I."

MONDAY'S CHILD

Monday's child
Is fair of face,
Tuesday's child
Is full of grace,
Wednesday's child
Is full of woe,
Thursday's child
Has far to go,

Friday's child
Is loving and and giving,
Saturday's child
Works hard for his living,
But the child that is born
On the Sabbath day
Is bonny and blithe,
And good and gay.

MARY, MARY,
QUITE CONTRARY

Mary, Mary,
Quite contrary,
How does your garden grow?
With cockle-shells,
And silver bells,
And pretty maids all in a row.

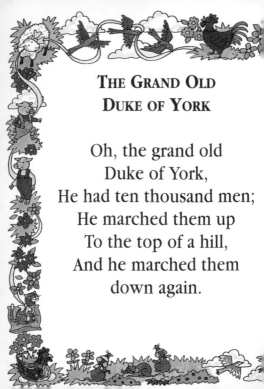

THE GRAND OLD DUKE OF YORK

Oh, the grand old
Duke of York,
He had ten thousand men;
He marched them up
To the top of a hill,
And he marched them
down again.

And when they were up,
they were up,
And when they were down,
they were down,
And when they were only
half way up,
They were neither up
nor down.

LITTLE MISS MUFFETT

Little Miss Muffett
Sat on a tuffet,
Eating her curds and whey;
There came a great spider,
And sat down beside her,
And frightened
Miss Muffett away.

THE LION AND THE UNICORN

The lion and the unicorn
Were fighting for the crown;
The lion beat the unicorn
All round the town.

Some gave them white bread,
And some gave them brown;
Some gave them plum-cake,
And drummed them out of town.

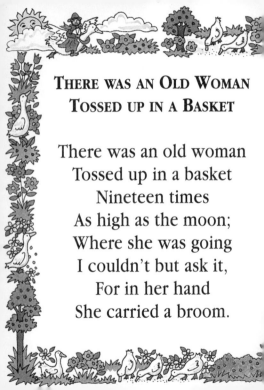

THERE WAS AN OLD WOMAN
TOSSED UP IN A BASKET

There was an old woman
Tossed up in a basket
Nineteen times
As high as the moon;
Where she was going
I couldn't but ask it,
For in her hand
She carried a broom.

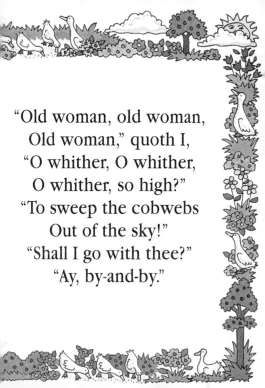

"Old woman, old woman,
Old woman," quoth I,
"O whither, O whither,
O whither, so high?"
"To sweep the cobwebs
Out of the sky!"
"Shall I go with thee?"
"Ay, by-and-by."

HUSH-A-BYE, BABY

Hush-a-bye, baby,
On the tree top;
When the wind blows,
The cradle will rock;
When the bough breaks,
The cradle will fall;
Down will come baby,
And cradle, and all.

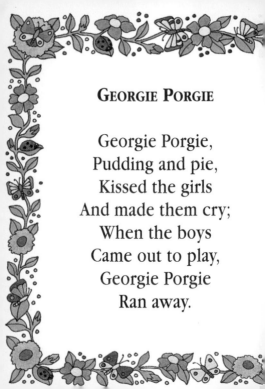

GEORGIE PORGIE

Georgie Porgie,
Pudding and pie,
Kissed the girls
And made them cry;
When the boys
Came out to play,
Georgie Porgie
Ran away.

PAT-A-CAKE

Pat-a-cake, pat-a-cake,
Baker's man!
Bake me a cake
As fast as you can:
Prick it and stick it,
And mark it with B,
And put it in the oven
For Baby and me.

THIS LITTLE PIG

This little pig went to market;
This little pig stayed at home;
This little pig had roast beef;
This little pig had none;
And this little pig cried,
"Wee, wee, wee!"
All the way home.

PUSSY-CAT, PUSSY-CAT

Pussy-cat, pussy-cat,
Where have you been?
I've been up to London
To look at the queen.
Pussy-cat, pussy-cat,
What did you there?
I frightened a little mouse
Under her chair.

JACK AND JILL

Jack and Jill
Went up the hill
To fetch a pail of water;
Jack fell down
And broke his crown,
And Jill came tumbling after.

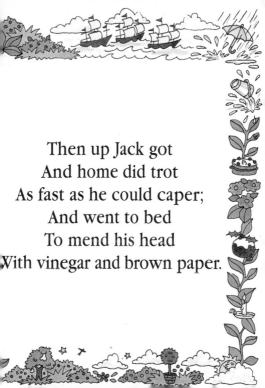

Then up Jack got
And home did trot
As fast as he could caper;
And went to bed
To mend his head
With vinegar and brown paper.

THERE WAS AN OLD WOMAN

There was an old woman
Who lived in a shoe;
She had so many children

She didn't know what to do;
She gave them some broth
Without any bread;
She whipped them all soundly
And put them to bed.

HICKETY PICKETY
MY BLACK HEN

Hickety Pickety,
My black hen,
She lays eggs
For gentlemen;
Sometimes nine,
And sometimes ten.
Hickety, Pickety,
My black hen!

OLD KING COLE

Old King Cole
Was a merry old soul,
And a merry old soul was he;
He called for his pipe,
And he called for his bowl,
And he called for his
fiddlers three.

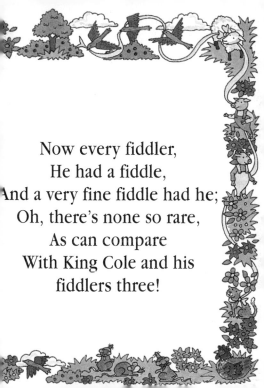

Now every fiddler,
He had a fiddle,
And a very fine fiddle had he;
Oh, there's none so rare,
As can compare
With King Cole and his
fiddlers three!

WEE WILLIE WINKIE

Wee Willie Winkie
Runs through the town,
Upstairs and downstairs
In his nightgown,
Rapping at the window,
Crying through the lock,
"Are the children in their beds,
For now it's eight o'clock?"

TWINKLE, TWINKLE, LITTLE STAR

Twinkle, twinkle, little star,
How I wonder what you are!
Up above the moon so high,
Like a diamond in the sky.

MATTHEW, MARK, LUKE, AND JOHN

Matthew, Mark,
Luke, and John,
Bless the bed
That I lie on!
Four corners to my bed,
Four angels round my head;
One to watch,
One to pray,
And two to bear
My soul away!

CHARLES PERRAULT

Mother Goose first came to life with Charles Perrault whose collection of folk tales (including *Cinderella*, *Puss in Boots* and *Sleeping Beauty*) was first published in France in 1697. The frontispiece showed an old woman telling a story to three children. On the wall nearby hung a plaque engraved with the words *Contes de Ma Mère l'Oye* or *Mother Goose's Tales*. It is widely believed that she represented a typical peasant woman who would have told such tales to amuse local children whilst watching over the village geese.

Thereafter, Mother Goose came to be associated with fairy tales and nursery rhymes and in 1833 a collection of rhymes was published in Boston, Massachusetts, under the name of *Mother Goose's Melodies*. It proved so popular that Mother Goose soon became accepted as the favourite "collector" of nursery rhymes.